DEAR MUMMY

love from

You teach us that we are important.

You teach us to trust.

to slow down.

You teach us that we are strong.

We teach you how strong you are.

You teach us that you would give up anything for us.

We teach you what you have gained.

You teach us about our world.

Dear Mummy Love From Us first published by **FROM YOU TO ME LTD**, in May 2022.

For a full range of our titles where gifts can also be personalised, please visit

WWW.FROMYOUTOME.COM

FROM YOU TO ME are committed to a sustainable future for our business, our customers and our planet. This book is printed and bound, in China, on FSC® certified paper.

Written and illustrated by Lucy Tapper & Steve Wilson fromlucy.com

All rights reserved. No part of this publication may be reproduced, stored in a retrieval system, or transmitted in any form or by any means electronic, mechanical, photocopying, recording, or otherwise, without the prior written permission of the copyright owner who can be contacted via the publisher at the above website address.

3   5   7   9   11   13   15   14   12   10   8   6   4   2

Copyright © 2022 **FROM YOU TO ME LTD**

ISBN 978-1-907860-95-9

Available titles in the range: Dear Mummy Love From Me, Dear Daddy Love From Me, Dear Mummy Love From Us & Dear Daddy Love From Us

FROM YOU TO ME LTD, STUDIO 100, THE OLD LEATHER FACTORY
GLOVE FACTORY STUDIOS, HOLT, WILTSHIRE, BA14 6RJ